BATMAN

SUPER DC HEROES

MAD HATTER'S
MOVIE
MADNESS

WRITTEN BY
DONALD LEMKE

ILLUSTRATED BY
GREGG SCHIGIEL AND
LEE LOUGHRIDGE

BATMAN CREATED BY
BOB KANE

www.raintreepublishers.co.uk
Visit our website to find out
more information about
Raintree books.

To order:
☎ Phone 0845 6044371
🖷 Fax +44 (0) 1865 312263
🖳 Email myorders@raintreepublishers.co.uk

Customers from outside the UK please telephone +44 1865 312262

Raintree is an imprint of Capstone Global Library Limited,
a company incorporated in England and Wales having its
registered office at 7 Pilgrim Street, London, EC4V 6LB
– Registered company number: 6695582

First published by Stone Arch Books in 2011
First published in hardback and paperback in the
United Kingdom by Capstone Global Library in 2011
The moral rights of the proprietor have been asserted.

Batman and all related characters, names, and elements
are trademarks of DC Comics © 2010.

Art Director: Bob Lentz
Designer: Brann Garvey
Production Specialist: Michelle Biedscheid
Editor: Vaarunika Dharmapala
Originated by Capstone Global Library Ltd
Printed and bound in China by Leo Paper Products Ltd

ISBN 978 1 406 22539 6 (hardback)
15 14 13 12 11
10 9 8 7 6 5 4 3 2 1

ISBN 978 1 406 22544 0 (paperback)
15 14 13 12 11
10 9 8 7 6 5 4 3 2 1

British Library Cataloguing in Publication Data
A full catalogue record for this book is
available from the British Library.

CONTENTS

CHAPTER 1

BIG SCREEN BRAINWASH

Tim Drake stepped out of a limousine in front of the Gotham City Cinema. Reporters lined the red carpet. **CLICK! CLICK!** They snapped photos of the city's most famous citizens. Through the blinding camera flashes, Tim looked up at the sign above the entrance. The title of the film, *The New Adventures of Alice in Wonderland 3-D*, glowed there in big, bright letters.

"What's wrong?" asked Bruce Wayne, following Tim out of the limo and giving him a shove. "Not used to the attention?"

"Ha!" Tim laughed. As the secret super heroes Batman and Robin, Bruce and Tim had faced far greater challenges than the paparazzi. "I just can't believe you got hold of tickets to the year's biggest premiere!"

"My company owns the cinema," replied the billionaire with a wink. "Now, come on. We're going to miss the previews."

Bruce and Tim hurried past the crowd and went inside. Except for a few people buying last-minute sweets and popcorn, the cinema's foyer was nearly empty.

"I knew we should've got here earlier," said Tim, starting to worry. "All the good seats are probably taken!" He grabbed Bruce by the elbow and pulled him towards the ticket counter. As they approached, the usher behind the counter grinned widely.

"Are we late?" Tim asked him.

For a moment, the usher stood in silence, adjusting the small hat on his head and continuing to smile. Then he reached into the pocket of his uniform and pulled out a giant watch.

"What a funny watch!" Tim exclaimed. "The hands are running backwards!"

The usher's grin quickly disappeared. "I've seen feet run, but never hands," he said with a serious face. "Perhaps you are the funny one."

"No, you don't understand," said Tim, trying to explain. "I meant that the time on your watch is counting down."

"Yes, but half the time it's counting *up*," the usher replied, holding out the watch to Bruce and Tim.

He pointed at the second hand, which was spinning anticlockwise. "See! On one side the hand goes down, and on the other side the hand goes up. I'd say it's counting round and round."

"What?" Tim asked. "No, I meant –"

"We're here for the premiere," Bruce interrupted, shoving the tickets at the strange man.

"Certainly," he replied. He took the tickets, slowly tore them both in half, and then returned the stubs. "But, of course, the screening has already started."

"Why didn't you say so?" Tim exclaimed. He grabbed Bruce again and dashed towards the main cinema.

"Wait!" shouted the usher as they left. "You've forgotten your 3-D glasses!"

Tim turned and stormed back to the counter. Gritting his teeth in frustration, he held out his hand. "Thank you," he grumbled.

"You wouldn't want to forget these," said the usher, handing Tim two pairs of plastic glasses. "I've heard the special effects are mind blowing!" **HAHAHAHA!**

As the usher's laugh echoed through the empty foyer, Bruce and Tim entered the darkened cinema. The previews had already started, and the audience stared up at the glowing screen. Each person wore a pair of the special 3-D glasses.

"There!" Tim whispered to Bruce, pointing at two empty seats in the middle of the second row. He ran down the aisle and quickly took his seat.

Bruce followed close behind. "Excuse me. Pardon me," said the billionaire, attempting to squeeze through the crowded row. "If I could just –"

CRUNCH! Bruce glanced down at the sticky floor. A pair of 3-D glasses had been crushed beneath his shoe. Suddenly, a little girl began to cry.

"Hey! Those were my daughter's glasses!" said an angry woman sitting next to the crying child.

"Sorry, madam," apologized Bruce. "Here! Take mine, little girl." He handed the child his own pair of 3-D glasses. She quickly stopped crying.

"But you'll miss the special effects," whispered Tim from his seat.

"Don't worry," said Bruce. "I'll get another pair." He turned and went back up the aisle.

In the foyer, Bruce stood at the deserted ticket counter and waited for the strange usher to return. But after few a moments, he decided to ask someone else for help.

"Excuse me," said Bruce, approaching the sweet counter. "Do you know where the man with the 3-D glasses went?"

"He just quit!" replied the annoyed boy behind the counter. "He said something about 'time' being up and then left. He was here for just one day!"

"Do you know if there are any extra glasses?" asked Bruce.

"He's probably left them by his old uniform," said the boy.

He pointed to a pile of crumpled clothes near the ticket counter. "Feel free to check," he said. "I have to get back to work."

Bruce quickly searched the area near the uniform. He lifted the usher's coat, gave it a shake, and set it back down. Then he noticed a silver name tag attached to the coat, etched with the initials "J.T."

For a moment, Bruce wondered what the initials stood for. Then a roar of laughter erupted from inside the main cinema.

"The film must have started!" Bruce said to himself.

He gave the area one last look and then rushed back inside the cinema – without a pair of 3-D glasses.

CHAPTER 2

A MAD TEA PARTY

Later that evening, as a thunderstorm gathered in the darkened sky, Bruce and Tim returned to Wayne Manor. Bruce Wayne's loyal butler, Alfred Pennyworth, greeted them at the mansion's front door.

"So how was the film, Master Tim?" asked Alfred, taking Tim's jacket and shaking off a few drops of rain.

Tim shrugged his shoulders. "Eh," he said, eyeing Bruce. "It was ... all right."

"Oh, come on," said Bruce.

The billionaire removed his coat and handed it to Alfred. "You're not going to hurt my feelings," he said. "Tell him what you really thought of the film."

"It was brilliant!" Tim exclaimed. "Possibly the best film of the year! Maybe even the greatest 3-D film of all time! And the special effects ... unbelievable."

"Okay, okay," said Bruce. "Now can we go to bed?"

"What's the matter, Master Bruce?" asked the butler.

Tim leant in towards Alfred. "He broke a kid's 3-D glasses and had to give her his pair," he explained.

"I chose to give her my glasses, Tim," Bruce interrupted. "And, by the way, you can probably take yours off now."

"No way," said Tim, adjusting his own 3-D glasses. "These are a collector's item. I can't wait to show them off at school." He sprinted up the spiral staircase to the first floor of the mansion. "Thanks again for the tickets, Bruce," he shouted down from his bedroom doorway.

Bruce stood at the bottom of the stairs, shaking his head. "Can you believe that, Alfred?" he said. "A grown boy attached to some cheap plastic glasses. Who would want such a silly souvenir?"

"Shall I search for another pair online, sir?" asked Alfred.

"You know me too well," said Bruce. He gave the loyal butler a pat on the back and went up the stairs. "Goodnight, Alfred."

"Goodnight, sir," he replied.

That night, as the city slept, a heavy rain pounded down on central Gotham. Far beneath the flooded streets, a man wearing a top hat and a bow tie paced back and forth inside an underground room filled with high-tech machinery. He reached into his purple overcoat, pulled out an oversized pocket watch, and smiled.

"Tick-tock," said the man, laughing. "It's almost time for the time I have planned!"

He scurried round the room, flipping switches and pulling levers on a giant control panel. Then he sat in front of a microphone and placed his hand over a glowing, red button. As his pocket watch started to chime, the man pressed down.

CLICK! "Wake up!" he screamed into the microphone. "The Mad Tea Party is about to begin!"

Meanwhile, back at Wayne Manor, an explosion of thunder rattled Tim's bedroom windows. The alarm clock on his bedside table showed that it was 11.59 p.m. in glowing, red numbers. Tim had dozed off nearly an hour ago, reading his favourite comic book and still wearing his clothes and 3-D glasses. The storm had not woken him, but then the clock struck midnight.

Tim's eyes opened wide, and he sprang up in bed. "I'm late! I'm late!" he shouted. **SPRONGG!** He bounced on to the floor and rushed out of the bedroom. "I shall be too late!"

Tim sprinted down the stairs and opened a door to a passage on the ground floor. At the bottom of another flight of stairs, he entered the Batcave, a secret storage room for the Dynamic Duo's equipment.

In a panic, Tim hopped on to a Batcycle, revved the motorbike's engine, and sped out of the cave towards Gotham City.

Within minutes, he arrived in central Gotham, skidding to a stop at the corner of Dodgson Avenue and Main Street. Tim quickly jumped off the Batcycle and waded through the ankle-deep puddles until he heard a hollow sound beneath his shoes. He knelt down and lifted off a manhole cover. *SPLASH!* A flood of dirty, brown water poured into the opening.

"I'm late! I'm late!" Tim repeated. Then he leapt into the deep, dark hole and landed in the dirty sewer water below. A maze of underground tunnels stretched out in every direction. But even in the dark, Tim somehow knew exactly which way to go.

Within moments, he spotted light coming from a small doorway at the end of a tunnel. Tim crept towards the tiny entrance, bent down, and peeked inside.

"Come in! Come in! There's plenty of room!" shouted a gap-toothed man in a large top hat. He was standing at the head of a long table, speaking into an oversized microphone. Dozens of guests surrounded the table, sipping tea from giant cups.

Tim slowly entered the room, which was filled with buzzing machinery. As he sat down in the last empty chair, the other guests turned their heads and stared at him with dazed eyes. Each person wore a pair of identical 3-D glasses.

"Every good crime begins with tea," said the man into the microphone.

The obedient guests turned their attention back to their host. "Well, 'crime' actually begins with C, doesn't it now?" he continued. "But, of course, I didn't bring you here to spell 'crime.' My spell brought you here to commit one."

With his microphone, the strange man walked over to a control panel and switched on a video monitor. **KLIKKK!** An image of a blonde woman suddenly appeared on the screen.

"To win the heart of my lovely Alice," shouted the madman, pointing to the video screen, "it will take a roomful of diamonds. And you will get them for me!"

Tim and the other guests stood up from the table, and together they replied, "Yes, master."

CHAPTER 3

BOY WONDER IN WONDERLAND

Later at Wayne Manor, an alarm rang in Bruce's bedroom. The billionaire woke up, threw on a dressing gown, and calmly walked down the corridor. An alarm at three o'clock in the morning would never startle Batman, the secret super hero. But when he arrived at Tim's bedroom, something did surprise him.

Tim was gone.

Bruce hurried down the spiral staircase and met Alfred on the ground floor. "Have you seen Tim?" he asked the butler.

"I assumed he was behind you, sir," Alfred replied. "You know how he likes to lie in."

"Not today," said Bruce, rushing through the secret passage to the Batcave.

As Bruce quickly changed into his Batsuit, Alfred checked the Batcomputer for information about the alarm. "Several jewellery shops in Gotham have been robbed, sir," said the butler. He turned and looked at the Batcycle's empty parking space. "And it appears Master Tim is already on the case."

Bruce approached the Batmobile and slid into the driver's seat. He switched on the vehicle's computer. The dashboard lit up with hundreds of buttons and several radar monitors. One screen displayed a map of central Gotham City.

Dozens of glowing, red lights on the screen showed the locations of each theft. A single yellow light blinked on and off near one of the markers.

"That's the Batcycle," said Batman, pointing at the yellow light. "You're right, Alfred. Tim must have got a head start."

"Perhaps this is his way of repaying you for the film tickets," the butler said.

Batman pressed a switch to open a secret exit. "Doesn't he know, Alfred," said the Dark Knight with a smile, "I do this stuff for free." Then he fired up the Batmobile's engine and raced out into the night.

Following his radar screen, Batman arrived at the corner of Dodgson and Main a short time later. He stepped out of the Batmobile and spotted the Batcycle.

As the Dark Knight approached the abandoned machine, he nearly fell into the open manhole Tim had uncovered a few hours earlier.

Batman knelt near the opening. Heavy rainwater continued to flood into the sewer below, washing away any clues, such as footprints or tool marks.

Splash! Splash! Over his shoulder, the Dark Knight heard a mob of young people dashing through the streets. "We're late! We're late!" they yelled. "This way!"

Batman spun around and squinted through the pouring rain. The mob was running towards him, away from Don's Jewellery Shop on the other side of the street. Each of them carried a large, black bag, and each wore a strange, animal face mask.

The Dark Knight leapt into the air.
A second later, he landed next to a boy
wearing a mask of a grinning cat. "Not so
fast," said Batman, snagging the crook by
the collar. He grabbed the boy's bag and
looked inside. It was filled with diamonds
and other valuable jewels. "Just as I
thought."

Batman pushed the cat-faced crook
aside and searched for the other thieves. He
spotted one, wearing the mask of a white
rabbit, about to escape down the manhole.
Without hesitating, the Dark Knight
reached into his Utility Belt, pulled out a
Batarang, and threw it at the thief. **FWIP!**
FWIP! A super-strong wire unravelled
behind the weapon and wrapped around
the thief's ankles. **THUD!** The crook fell
face-first on to the flooded road.

Batman walked to the fallen criminal. He crouched on the wet asphalt and turned the crook on to his back. "Let's see who you really are," said the Dark Knight. He grabbed the rabbit mask and pulled it off.

"Tim?" exclaimed Batman.

Tim stood up and looked round in a daze. Behind him, the other masked crooks were jumping into the open manhole, escaping through the sewers.

Before Batman could react, Tim grabbed the mask from the ground. He ripped off one of the rabbit ears and placed the mask back on his face. Then he turned and leapt into the manhole.

A moment later, the Dark Knight went down after him, never once considering the danger he was getting into.

CHAPTER 4

DOWN THE RABBIT HOLE

Down, down, down, Batman fell through the manhole and splashed into the sewer below. When he looked up, Tim and the other crooks were gone.

The Dark Knight stared at his hand. He was still holding the torn piece of mask. "A rabbit ear," Batman said to himself. "What was Tim trying to tell me?"

The World's Greatest Detective rubbed the piece between his fingers. He could see that the mask had been made from several layers of heavy-duty cardboard.

Between the layers, Batman felt a pattern of thin ridges, like the veins of a leaf. He pulled at the rain-soaked edges of the cardboard, slowly separating each layer. In the middle, Batman found a web of wires connected to a tiny microchip.

"I should have known," said the Dark Knight, recognizing the technology. He thought about the faces of the masks again. A grinning cat. A dormouse. A white rabbit. Characters from the book *Alice's Adventures in Wonderland.* "This can be the work of only one man." *CRUNCH!* Batman crushed the sparking microchip in his wet glove. "The Mad Hatter," he growled.

Batman had faced the villain many times before. He knew the Mad Hatter used this type of device to brainwash innocent victims into committing crimes.

"How could he have brainwashed Tim?" the Dark Knight asked himself. "I was with him the whole time at the cinema."

Then Batman recalled the strange usher. His gap-toothed smile and puzzling riddles suddenly made sense. "Of course!" shouted the Dark Knight. He remembered the initials "J.T." etched on the usher's name tag. Now Batman knew that the letters stood for "Jervis Tetch," the true identity of the Mad Hatter.

"Jervis must have installed his brainwashing microchips into the 3-D glasses," concluded Batman. "So the special effects really *were* mind blowing."

Then suddenly, the Dark Knight heard a loud rumbling coming from behind him. The ground beneath his feet began to shake.

Batman spun around, expecting to see an underground train barrelling down the tunnel. Instead, he saw a wall of storm water crashing towards him. **WHOOOOSH!**

The wave knocked Batman off his feet. Within a moment, he was up to his chin in dirty water, swirling through the sewers. He tried to stop himself by digging his gloves into the wall. Sparks flew from his fingertips, but the rushing water pulled him deeper into the tunnels.

Barely able to breathe, Batman reached into his Utility Belt. He pulled out his grapnel gun, aimed at a sewer pipe above him, and fired. **CLANK!** The metal grapnel hook latched on to the pipe. The Dark Knight quickly pushed the Recoil button on the gun, and a super-strong wire pulled him safely out of the water.

Batman suddenly spotted one of the masked criminals dangling from the ceiling. He was sitting on a nearby sewer pipe, wearing the mask of a grinning Cheshire cat.

"Where's the Mad Hatter?" shouted the Dark Knight.

The cat-faced crook pointed further down the tunnels. "In that direction," said the masked thief, "lives a Hatter."

"Which way?" asked Batman, frustrated by the situation. The super hero knew he could not harm the brainwashed youth, but he needed more information.

"That depends on which way you want to go," the boy replied.

"It doesn't matter which way," said Batman. "As long as I get there."

"Oh, you're sure to do that," said the cat-faced crook with a laugh, "if you only walk long enough." The brainwashed boy jumped from the pipe and splashed into the tunnel below.

By now, the rushing water had passed, and was shallow enough to wade through again. Batman quickly released his grapnel gun. He landed in the tunnel and took off behind the cat-faced crook, following his splashes through the pitch-black darkness.

A short time later, the noises stopped. The boy had somehow disappeared.

Batman continued slowly down the tunnel until he reached a dead end. "Where did he go?" the Dark Knight asked himself. He felt the stone wall in front of him, searching for a secret passage.

Then near his feet, he spotted the top of a tiny doorway, nearly hidden in the dirty, brown water. Batman knelt and opened the door. As water spilled into the opening, the Dark Knight held his breath and crawled inside.

On the other side of the door, Batman stood and listened. The room was silent and dark. But then, before he could turn on his night-vision lenses, the lights suddenly came on. **CLICK!**

Batman was surround by dozens of brainwashed people, each wearing a different cardboard mask. And, in the middle of them all, stood their leader, the Mad Hatter.

"Welcome," shouted the crazy criminal, "to my Mad Tea Party!"

CHAPTER 5

OFF WITH THEIR HEADS!

"Thanks for the invitation, Hatter, but I have other plans!" replied Batman. He lunged at the crazed super-villain.

"Get him!" shouted the Mad Hatter into his microphone.

The brainwashed crowd obeyed their master. A dormouse, a Cheshire cat, and other masked characters leapt at Batman and quickly tackled him to the ground. The Dark Knight tried to get up, throwing people left and right. **POW! SLAM!** Soon, however, he stopped.

These are innocent people, thought Batman. *I have to capture the Mad Hatter without hurting them.*

The Mad Hatter looked amused by his foe's lack of effort. "What's the matter?" he said. "Giving up so soon?"

"You'll never get away with this, Hatter," said Batman.

"Oh, really?" replied the crazy crook. The Mad Hatter waved his hand, and the obedient crowd parted. Behind them, a large rubbish skip was completely filled with diamonds and other jewels. "It appears that I already have, Batman."

The Mad Hatter walked to the skip and dug out a fistful of gems. "You see," continued the villain, "with these diamonds, I'll win back my beloved Alice."

"And then," he continued, "we'll rule all of Gotham. The King and Queen of Hearts!"

While the Mad Hatter spouted his crazy plan, Batman scanned the room. He searched for a way out of the situation, but time was quickly ticking away.

Suddenly, Batman spotted something that made him smile. Through the crowd, he saw a single rabbit ear poking above the other masks. *Tim*, he thought.

Batman quickly turned his attention back to the Mad Hatter. "That's a great plan, Hatter, but there's one little problem," said the super hero. "Alice will never take you back."

"And why not?" shouted the villain.

"Because you're mad!" replied Batman.

"Don't you think I know that?" squealed the Mad Hatter. He spread his arms and looked around the room. "I'm mad. You're mad. We're all mad here!" *HAHAHAHA!*

Suddenly, Tim jumped out from behind
the crowd and pulled off his mask. "Speak
for yourself!" he shouted. "Now, Batman –
off with their heads!"

The Dark Knight followed his partner's lead. The Dynamic Duo circled the room, snatching the masks off each of the brainwashed victims. Within seconds, the tables had turned, and the Mad Hatter was now the one outnumbered.

"Nooooo!" the villain screamed. He threw his microphone on to the floor and made a break for the exit.

No longer under his spell, the mob surrounded the crook. The crowd had remembered everything that had happened while they were brainwashed. They were not about to let the villain get away.

A few minutes later, Batman led the crowd through the sewers to the open manhole. The rain had stopped, and the Gotham City police had arrived to help people back on to the street.

Once everyone else was safe, Batman climbed up the hole with his prisoner. He handed over the Mad Hatter to the officers. "Let him watch the sunrise," Batman said, pointing towards the horizon. "It might be the last one he sees for a while."

The Dark Knight turned and walked over to his sidekick. "Okay, Tim," started Batman. "I think I've worked out what happened. Hatter installed his devices into the 3-D glasses, brainwashing everyone at the cinema – except me, of course. Then he installed the same microchips in the masks, which is why you robbed the jewellery shop."

Tim nodded.

"But, when I pulled off your mask here on the street," Batman continued, "the spell was broken, is that right?"

Tim nodded again.

"Then I have only one question for you," asked the Dark Knight. "Why didn't you tell me you were no longer brainwashed?"

"I didn't want the Mad Hatter to know his plan had been foiled," Tim replied. "At least not until you reached his hideout."

"Good thinking," said Batman. "Patience is a sign of a mature hero."

"And," Tim added with a smile, "You never got to see the 3-D *Alice in Wonderland* film. I thought this way you'd get to star in your own version!"

Mad Hatter

REAL NAME: Jervis Tetch

OCCUPATION: Professional criminal

BASE: Gotham City

HEIGHT:
1 m 42 cm

WEIGHT:
67 kg

EYES:
Black

HAIR:
Black

Jervis Tetch is obsessed with Lewis Carroll's book, *Alice's Adventures in Wonderland*. He believes himself to be the Mad Hatter, a crazy hat maker from Carroll's book, and has taken the name as his own. Tetch is also convinced that Alice, a former co-worker, is the main character from *Wonderland*, and that she is destined to marry him. This belief has led Tetch to create mind control technology in order to brainwash Alice, as well as the rest of the world, into living out his crazy fantasy.

G.C.P.D. GOTHAM CITY POLICE DEPARTMENT

- True to his super-villain name, the Mad Hatter is obsessed with hats of all shapes and sizes. His crimes are often hat-themed or involve stealing expensive headwear.

- Tetch is obsessed with the book Alice's Adventures in Wonderland, as well as its sequel, Through the Looking Glass. Tetch loves these stories so much that he cannot tell the difference between Wonderland and the real world.

- The Mad Hatter has created several inventions that place other people's minds under his control. He often plants them in hats of varying kinds to catch his victims unprepared. He has also concealed them inside electronic devices, like radios and mobile phones, to spread his mind control powers across entire cities.

- Tetch's mind control technology can make his victims stronger, faster, and tougher, thereby turning them into fearsome servants.

CONFIDENTIAL

BIOGRAPHIES

Donald Lemke works as a children's book editor and writer. He is the author of the Zinc Alloy graphic novel adventure series. He also wrote *Captured Off Guard*, a World War II story, and a graphic novelization of *Gulliver's Travels*. Most recently, he has written several Batman adventures for DC Super Heroes chapter books.

Gregg Schigiel has wanted to be a cartoonist since he was 11 years old. He has worked on projects featuring Batman, Spider-Man, SpongeBob SquarePants, and just about everything in between.

Lee Loughridge has been working in comics for more than fifteen years. He currently lives in a tent on the beach.

GLOSSARY

3-D glasses glasses which allow you to watch a film as though the action was happening right in front of you. *3-D* stands for three-dimensional (having length, breadth, and depth).

brainwash make someone accept and believe something

foe enemy

foil prevent someone from doing something successfully

microchip very thin device with electronic circuits printed on it. Microchips are used in computers and other electronic equipment.

obedient do what you are told to do

paparazzi photographers who follow celebrities around to take pictures of them

usher someone who shows people to their seats in a theatre or cinema

Utility Belt Batman's belt, which holds all of his weaponry and gadgets

DISCUSSION QUESTIONS

1. Which half of the Dynamic Duo did more to defeat the Mad Hatter – Robin or Batman? Why?

2. This book has ten illustrations. Which one is your favourite? Why?

3. Tim Drake's secret identity is Robin. Should a super hero keep his or her true identity a secret? Why or why not?

WRITING PROMPTS

1. Imagine that you are the new Robin. As Batman's partner, what skills would you bring to the team? Write about it.

2. Robin goes undercover to stop the Mad Hatter. Imagine that you are an undercover detective. What kinds of crimes would you solve?

3. The Mad Hatter invents devices that help him commit crimes. Create your own invention. What is its name? What does it do? Write about your device. Then draw a picture of it.